Jenny COLGAN

POLLY AND THE PUFFIN

L B

THE STORMY DAY

LITTLE, BROWN BOOKS FOR YOUNG READERS

First published in Great Britain in 2016 by Hodder and Stoughton

1 3 5 7 9 10 8 6 4 2

Text copyright © Jenny Colgan, 2016
Illustrations copyright © Thomas Docherty, 2016 (based on characters originated by Jenny Colgan)

The moral rights of the author and illustrator have been asserted.

A CIP catalogue record for this book
is available from the British Library.

ISBN 9780349131924

Printed in Italy

Little, Brown Books for Young Readers
An imprint of
Hachette Children's Group
Part of Hodder and Stoughton
Carmelite House
50 Victoria Embankment
London EC4Y 0DZ

An Hachette UK Company
www.hachette.co.uk

www.hachettechildrens.co.uk

*For my patient D: on sunny days
and stormy days and all the days.*

It was a special day for Polly. She woke up early, and she and her puffin friend, Neil, started dancing the funky boogaloo to their favourite song on the radio.

Mummy was trying to do Busy Stuff.

"Come and dance!" said Polly,
loudly.

"Can you just give me five minutes?"
said Mummy. (Does your mummy ever
say that?)

So Polly and Neil had a go on their adventure playground.

And made themselves some breakfast.
(Neil liked tuna on his cereal.)

Then they saved the fishing
boats from Evil Rubber Duckie.

"We have done EVERYTHING!" said Polly. "It MUST be time now."

"It's only half past seven in the morning," said Mummy (which is very, very early).

"But you are busy and we are just waiting."

"Eep," said Neil.

"I see that," said Mummy.

"Because! Daddy is coming home on his fishing boat today! I want to see him!" cried Polly.

"I want to see Daddy too. That's why I'm trying to finish my work."

Mummy said Polly and Neil could
go outside, in front of the little house by
the sea, where she could keep an eye on
them.

"Boots on!" said Polly, pulling on her
bright, shiny, spotty wellington boots.

Then she looked at her feet.

Then she took her boots off and put them on again the right way round.

"Eep," said Neil.

"Neil and I will do 'eeping' about waiting on our special day."

They hopped on to the wall and hopped off again. They counted the masts of the boats jangling on the water, then counted them again because the number was TOO BIG. (Can you count them?)

But mostly, Polly stared out — past the wall, past the lighthouse, past the boats in the harbour and far away to the deep blue sea — and wondered where her daddy was.

Once she thought she saw his boat, but it was only a seagull in the distance. Polly and Neil didn't play with seagulls.

The boat masts jangled louder and
louder. Above their heads, black clouds
began to gather. Polly shivered, and then
the rain started to fall: *plop, plop, plop*.

"Polly! Come inside!" called Mummy.

"You have to say, 'Polly and Neil, come inside!'" shouted Polly, getting wet.

Suddenly, Polly heard an "eep".
She turned around and Neil was high
up in the air, flying round and round,
higher and higher, and straight over
the sea into the big black clouds
of the storm.

NEiL !!

"MUMMY! Where's Neil going? He's
flying into the storm! Maybe he doesn't
know he'll get ALL WET."

"It's all right for birds to get wet,"
said Mummy. "Let's go inside, and we'll
take a look at his feather."

Polly fetched the special puffin feather Neil had given her.

She brought her toy, Wrong Puffin, downstairs too, just in case. She didn't like to think of Neil out in the storm by himself. She didn't like to think of anybody being out in the storm.

"See how it's all oily and coated?" said
Polly's mummy, looking at the feather.
"That keeps Neil safe and dry."

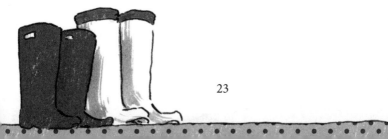

"Will Daddy be safe and dry in the storm?" asked Polly anxiously.

The lightning crackled and rattled around them, and Mummy held Polly nice and tight.

"Daddy knows lots and lots and lots about boats. And he's been in plenty of storms. So don't worry."

"I wouldn't like to be lost in a storm," said Polly.

"You never would be," said her mummy. "I would come and find you. That's what mummies do. Shelter you from storms."

And Mummy smiled and gave Polly a big cuddle, like this one I am giving you now.

Polly looked out
at the lighthouse,
which had come on
even though it was
still the daytime. The
light went round and
round.

"Will the lighthouse help Daddy?" said Polly.

"Of course," said her mummy. "Lighthouses shine out in the dark. To bid sailors safe passage and show them the way home."

Polly wasn't sure about this. It was VERY stormy.

Polly tried to play with Wrong Puffin
to help the time pass, but it wasn't the
same as playing with Neil.

Nobody was fighting with Evil Rubber
Duckie.

Wrong Puffin didn't want any cereal. He didn't even want a lollipop.

And Neil missed the fluffy towels coming out of the drier!

Outside, the storm grew stronger and stronger. There was still no Daddy and still no Neil. Even Mummy was standing at the window now.

"Waiting is hard," said Polly, taking her mummy's hand.

"Yes it is," said Mummy.

Polly and Mummy started to bake Neil's favourite seed cake but Polly was watching the lighthouse go round, and she spilled all the raisins.

They tried to make a Neil out of play-dough but it went all brown and didn't look anything like a puffin.

Polly got very cross. When her favourite song came on the radio, she didn't feel like dancing one tiny bit. Instead, she took the play-dough and threw it on the floor.

Polly and her mummy looked at each other.

Finally Mummy said, "Let's get out of the house!"

So they went out in the rain and walked to the bakery. They were blown the whole way!

"I am waiting for my daddy and I am waiting for Neil and I am very cross," said Polly, crossly, to the nice lady in the bakery. "It is taking a long time for them to come home."

"Oh dear," said the bakery lady. "Would a cinnamon bun help?"

"Hmmph," said Polly.

"I think what you meant to say was 'yes please, thank you very much'," said Polly's mummy.

"Yespleasethankyouverymuch," said Polly.

"How's it going?" said the bakery lady to Polly's mummy, pouring her a cup of coffee.

"Perfect, as you can see," she replied.

Polly ate her bun and felt a bit better. The raindrops were making pretty patterns on the windows.

"I'm sorry about the play-dough and the raisins," she said.

"That's OK," said Mummy. "Look around. It's not just you. Everybody is waiting."

Polly looked. All around
the bakery people were looking
at their watches and fiddling
with their phones and
staring out to sea.

"Are they waiting for
puffins and daddies?"
said Polly.

"Well, they're all
waiting for someone,"
said her mummy.

"Even the grown-ups?"
"Even the grown-ups."

"Do they feel sad too?"

Polly's mummy lifted Polly up onto her lap.

"It is always sad when people you love are far away," she said, "whether you are big or small."

"Or medium like me," said Polly.

"Or medium like you," said Mummy.

"It's all right, Mummy," said Polly. "I am RIGHT HERE. And so is Wrong Puffin. Although he's not much use."

"You know," said the bakery lady, "after the rain falls, the sun always comes out. I promise. Would you like to take an extra cinnamon bun to share with Neil when he comes home?"

"Yes please," said Polly.

She and her mummy walked out onto the cobbles, where Polly looked into the distance through the rain.

Suddenly, one ray of sun broke
through the clouds.

And the rain was not so heavy.

And she could see a tiny dot.

And the tiny dot got bigger . . . and bigger . . . and bigger. Until she could see it was . . .

"Neil!" shouted Polly in delight.

"EEP!" said Neil, and he landed on her shoulder before pecking in her pocket until he found the cinnamon bun. Then he let Polly scratch his head, because they had missed each other very much.

But that was not all. Behind Neil, sailing out of the storm, was the fleet of fishing boats.

And after all the waiting and the cereal and the play-dough and the buns, there, at the little house by the sea, was a very wet, tired-looking man, holding an oily puffin feather.

It was Polly's daddy.

"Neil was leading Daddy out of the storm, wasn't he?" said Polly later, when they were all warm and cosy and dry and eating fish and chips by the fire.

Polly's mummy and daddy looked at one another.

"You know," said Polly's
mummy, "I really think he was."

Daddy tucked Polly in, with Wrong Puffin and her feather. Neil had gone back to his nest.

"Thank you for looking after Mummy for me while I was away," he said, kissing her on the forehead.

"That's OK," said Polly. "Neil helped."

Outside, the rain after the storm
fell softly on the little house by the sea.
And everybody slept.

POLLY AND NEIL ♥ LOVE ♥

. . . lighthouses!

In this story the lighthouse is very important. Turn the page to see what Polly and Neil know about lighthouses.

A lighthouse is a tower with a bright light at the top, normally built on a clifftop to help sailors find their way (and to help them keep their boats away from rocks).

The tallest lighthouse in the world is more than ONE HUNDRED times taller than Polly, even when she is standing on her tiptoes!

Each lighthouse used to
have a lighthouse keeper
to light the lamp each
evening, and turn it
off during the daytime.
Now, most lighthouses
have automatic lights,
powered by electricity.

Lighthouses are normally tall, white and
circular. But they can be many shapes
and sizes. There are square ones, short
ones, octagonal ones . . . If you were
going to build a lighthouse, what would it
look like?

RECIPES

Polly and Neil's Favourite Seed Cake

This is the cake that Polly and her mummy try to make in the story – but Polly spills all the raisins!

If you're not keen on the taste of caraway seeds, you could use a different seed instead. You'll need a grown-up to help, especially with putting the cake in the oven.

INGREDIENTS

- 175g butter or margarine
- 175g caster sugar
- 3 medium eggs
- 250g self-raising flour

- 38g caraway seeds
- 75g raisins
- 2tbsp milk

You'll also need a 1kg loaf tin, buttered and lined with baking paper.

INSTRUCTIONS

1. This is an "all-in-one" cake which means you just put all the ingredients into a bowl at the same time! Beat the mixture with a wooden spoon until smooth.

2. Put the mixture into the loaf tin and bake at 160°C for 45 minutes to an hour. The cake is done when a skewer comes out clean from the centre.

3. Leave the cake to cool in the tin for 10 minutes, and then transfer to a wire rack.

4. Polly likes to eat a slice of cake with a glass of milk to drink!

Peppermint Lighthouses

Real lighthouses help to guide sailors out at
sea, but these peppermint versions are just
as useful . . . for your tummy! If you're not
keen on peppermint, you could try using
vanilla essence instead.

INGREDIENTS

- 200g icing sugar

- 100g condensed milk

- Peppermint essence

- Food colouring – your choice of colour!

- 2 bowls

- A wooden spoon

- A baking tray or plate, lined with baking
  paper or tin foil

INSTRUCTIONS

1. Take two bowls, and put half the condensed milk in each bowl.

2. Add a couple of drops of peppermint essence to each bowl.

3. Into just one bowl, add a couple of drops of food colouring.

4. Sieve 100g of icing sugar into each bowl and use a wooden spoon to mix — you should end up with quite a stiff doughy mixture, so sprinkle more sugar if the mixture is too sticky.

Create your lighthouses on your baking tray by taking a little ball of the white mixture and rolling it into a short cylinder shape, then doing the same with a slightly smaller ball of the coloured mixture to place on top as the next layer.

6 Your lighthouse can be as tall as you like – Polly likes to have five stripes for hers! Your final piece needs to be a bit pointy at the top so it looks like a real lighthouse.

7 Leave your lighthouses to harden in the fridge for an hour before you eat them.

RHYMES

Rainy Day Rhymes are perfect for singing as you splash through puddles. Do you recognise any of Polly's favourite ones?

Incy Wincy spider climbed up the water spout,

Down came the rain and washed the spider out.

Out came the sunshine and dried up all the rain,

And Incy Wincy spider climbed up the spout again.

I hear thunder, I hear thunder.

Hark don't you? Hark don't you?

Pitter, patter raindrops,

Pitter, patter raindrops,

I'm wet through; so are you.

I see blue skies, I see blue skies,

Way up high, way up high!

Hurry up the sunshine,

Hurry up the sunshine,

We'll soon dry! We'll soon dry!

ACTIVITIES

Making Play-Dough

Sometimes it's raining outside and it feels like there's nothing to do at home. But with this fun activity, the time will whizz by! Ask a grown-up to help you as it can get a little messy . . .

You will need:

- A cup for measuring

- A bowl for mixing

- 1 cup of salt

- 2 cups of flour

- 1 cup of water

- Optional: food colouring, paint

How to make the dough:

1. Put the salt and the flour in the bowl and add half a cup of the water. Get mixing! With hands is best, although it can be a bit messy . . .

2. Slowly add a little bit more water. You might not need it all! You want the dough to be squidgy, but not too sticky or it will be hard to make it into shapes. (If you accidentally add too much water, try adding a sprinkle more flour.)

3. If you would like to, you can add a few drops of food colouring at this stage to make a pale-coloured dough. Or you can paint later on — see over the page for tips!

4. Now, sprinkle some flour on your table (or use some baking parchment) and make anything you like from the salt dough.

Decorating Tips

You can roll the dough flat using a rolling pin, and then cut out shapes using cookie cutters. Can you make a puffin with these shapes?

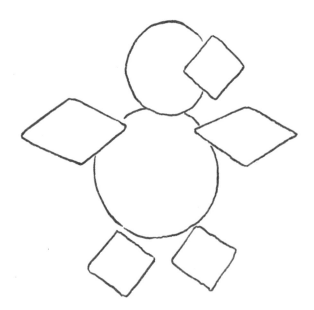

If you use a pencil to make a hole before you dry them out, you can hang them up as decorations.

Dry your shapes overnight (or in the oven at a very low temperature with the help of a grown-up!) and then paint them in fun colours. If you made a puffin, can you give it black wings and an orange beak?

Colouring in
Polly and Neil

Making Boats for the Bath

Polly's daddy is a fisherman, and Polly loves boats too! She likes to make her own to float in the bathtub. Ask a grown-up to help you make one too.

You will need:

- A little tub (either plastic or foil – you can use the ones from takeaway meals, or even an empty margarine tub!)
- A lolly stick
- A piece of thick paper or card
- Glue
- Blue tack/plasticine/play-dough
- Pens or pencils and other decorating materials
- Scissors

How to make your boat:

1 First you need to make your sail. Fold your paper in half and then draw a shape right on the fold. Polly likes her sails to be triangles, but you could have a square — or anything you like really.

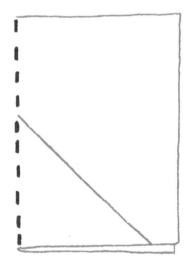

2 Get a grown-up to help you cut out your sail (so it will still have the fold down one side) then decorate it.

Now, use the glue to stick your lolly stick inside, next to the fold — make sure there's plenty sticking out as this will be the mast.

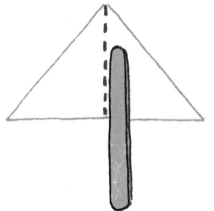

 Take your tub and put a blob of blue tack or plasticine in the bottom.

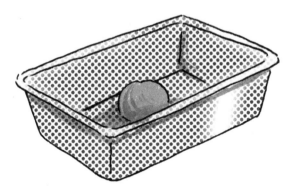

Add your sail.

Now you have a boat to float in the bathtub!
(Tip: WATCH OUT for Evil Rubber
Duckies!)

Jenny Colgan is best known for writing bestselling novels for grown-ups including *Meet Me at the Cupcake Café* and *Welcome to Rosie Hopkins' Sweetshop of Dreams.* But when a feathery character from *Little Beach Street Bakery* caught her readers' attention she knew he needed a story of his own . . .

Thomas Docherty is an acclaimed author and illustrator of children's picture books including

Little Boat, *Big Scary Monster* and *The Driftwood Ball*. *The Snatchabook*, which was written by his wife Helen, has been shortlisted for several awards in the UK and the US and translated into 17 languages. He loves going into schools and helping kids to write their own stories. Thomas lives in Wales by the sea with his wife and two young daughters, so he had plenty of inspiration when it came to illustrating *Polly and the Puffin*.

Neil has a cameo in Jenny's next book for grown-ups, *The Little Shop of Happy Ever After*, as well as having another book of his own in 2017.

Have you read Polly and Neil's first book?

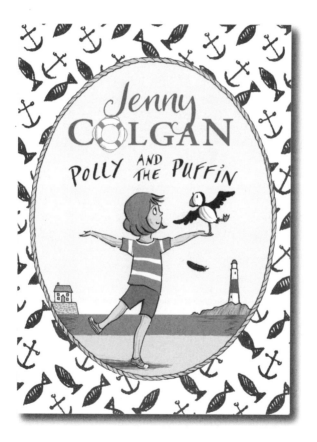